The animals have to... ...
They are afraid because their hom...
...polluted by people who don't kn...
...are. These people don't know that...
...isters and Brothers. They cut d...
...garbage in my oceans and rivers,...
...with pollution.

Where will the animals live when...
...gone? Where will the dolphins and s...
...oceans are too dirty to live in? An...
...fly when my sky is poisoned?

Imagine what life would be li...
...living on me. What if there were n...
...Africa? No tigers in India? No...
...No penguins in Antarctica? No...
Imagine my oceans with no w...
...swimming in them. And all th...
...gone.

...

Dear Children
of the Earth

A letter from Home

Schim Schimmel

NorthWord
PRESS, INC

Minocqua, Wisconsin

Dear Children of the Earth,

I am writing this letter to ask for your help. Do you know who I am? I am the planet, earth. But I am much more than just a planet. I am your Home. I am your Mother Earth. And just like you, there is only one of me, so I am very special. I need to be loved and cared for, just like you.

Heavenly Earth

Let me tell you more about myself. I am the boulders and trees

you love to climb. I am the wet sand at the beach that squishes under

your bare feet. I am the grass you lie down on when you look up

at my clouds. I am the rivers and lakes and oceans you love to swim in.

I am the cool green forests, the hot red deserts, and the cold white glaciers.

I love to hug you with my warm sunshine, tickle you with my wind,

and kiss you with my rain.

Paradise Lost

Passage to Home

Now let me ask you something. When you look in the mirror, what do you see? You see your eyes, of course. You see your hair, your nose, and your mouth. And if you smile, you see your teeth.

Do you know what I see when I look in the mirror? I see all the animals walking on my land. I see all the birds flying in my sky. I see all the fishes, whales, and dolphins swimming in my oceans. And all of these animals I see are my children.

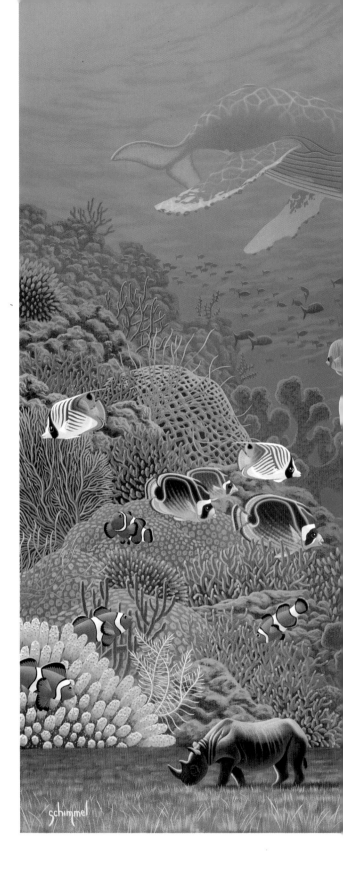

But there is something else I see
when I look in the mirror. I see all of
you! I see you because you, too, are
my children.

All of the animals that live on me
are your sisters and brothers!
We are all one big family.

But many people still don't know
they are my children, and that all of
the animals are their sisters and
brothers. They still don't know that
we are one big family.

Between Two Worlds

The animals have told me, "We are worried, Mother Earth.
We are afraid because our homes are being destroyed by people who
don't know better, or don't care. They don't know that we are their
sisters and brothers. Mother Earth, these people are cutting down your
forests, dumping garbage in your oceans and rivers, and filling your
sky with pollution."

Tell me, my children, where will the animals live when my forests are all
gone? Where will the whales and dolphins swim when my oceans are too
dirty to live in? And where will the birds fly when my sky is poisoned?

Earth Song

Final Embrace

Arrival

Imagine what life would be like with no wild animals living on me.

What if there were no elephants left in Africa? No tigers in India?

No pandas in China?

Dance of the Humpbacks

What if there were no penguins in Antarctica?

No kangaroos in Australia?

No grizzly bears in the United States?

Giver of Life

Imagine my oceans with no whales or dolphins swimming in them, and all the seals and sea otters gone. Imagine how empty my blue sky would look with no birds flying. And think how quiet the trees would be with no birds singing. I would be so lonely. Wouldn't you be lonely, too?

Mother to Mother

And so, my children, I need your help. And the animals need your help, too.
"But Mother Earth," you ask, "how can I help you and all my sister and
brother animals when you are so big, and I am so small?"

Well, my children, let me tell you something. I am not so big. As a matter of fact, I am quite small. When you go outside at night and look up at all the millions and millions of stars, you will see how small I really am. Compared to the night sky, I am no bigger than you!

Only One Home

But because I look so big, people think I don't know what they do to me.

They think I can't feel what they do to me.

But I do know.

And I do feel.

Ancient Wisdom

My children, when many people do a little thing to me, it becomes a big thing. So it's very important for each person to stop doing things that hurt me, or hurt their sister and brother animals.

Born of the Stars

Serengeti Soul

Remember, there is only one of me, but there are billions of people. So when each person does a little something to help me, it makes a very big difference. A very good difference.

The Waiting

In Search of His Future

Now what do you think is the biggest, most important thing you can do to help me? What do you think I need from you more than anything else in the world? I will tell you.

I need you to love me. That's all. Just love me as much as I love you.
Because when you love me, you will care for me. And when you care for me,
you will protect me. And when you care for me and protect me, you will save
your Home, and the homes of your sister and brother animals.

Candle in the Window

Where are My Brothers?

My children, tell your friends and other people what I have told you. Tell them I am their only Home, and that I need them to love me and care for me. Tell them all the animals are their sisters and brothers, and that we are all one big family. And tell them, too, that I always know when they do little things to help me.

Lair of the Snow Leopard

My dear children of the earth, I will now end my letter to you. Remember,

I am your Home. And just like you, there is only one of me. If you love me,

care for me, and protect me, I will always be your Home. Forever and ever.

I love you with all my heart,

Mother Earth

Dear Children of the Earth,
by Schim Schimmel

Schim Schimmel has been a professional artist and
musician for several years. He studied watercolor and
oil painting, but now prefers to work with acrylics.
All the original paintings from the pages of this book
were done in acrylics. To emphasize his own concern
for the environment, Schimmel began writing lyrics
and stories to accompany his unique art work.
Dear Children of the Earth is the result of combining
these two creative talents into one powerful piece.

© 1994 Schim Schimmel

Originally published in Japan in 1993 by Shogakukan, Inc.

Edited by Greg Linder
Cover Design: Russell S. Kuepper
Book Design: Kazuo Kuribayashi and Yoko Mori for The Studio Tokyo Japan, Inc.
Art Direction: Yukimasa Okumura for The Studio Tokyo Japan, Inc.

Published by
NorthWord Press, Inc.
P.O. Box 1360
Minocqua, WI 54548

Library of Congress Cataloging-in-Publication Data
Schimmel, Schimm.
    Dear Children of the earth / by Schimm Schimmel.
        p.   cm.
    ISBN 1-55971-225-2
    [1. Earth—Fiction. 2. Environmental protection—Fiction.
    3. Letters—Fiction.] I. Title.
    PZ7.S346325De   1993   93-47672
    [E]—dc20   CIP

For a free catalog describing NorthWord's line of
audio products, nature books and calendars, call 1-800-356-4465.

Printed in Singapore

The animals have told me, "W
They are afraid because their hom
r polluted by people who don't k
care. These people don't know that
Sisters and Brothers. They cut o
garbage in my oceans and rivers
with pollution.

Where will the animals live whe
gone? Where will the dolphins and
oceans are too dirty to live in? A
fly when my sky is poisoned?

Imagine what life would be li
living on me. What if there were
Africa? No tigers in India? No
No penguins in Antarctica? No
Imagine my oceans with no
swimming in them. And all th
gone.

And imagine how empty my